Emilie:

La Marquise Du Châtelet Defends Her Life Tonight

by Lauren Gunderson

A Samuel French Acting Edition

SAMUELFRENCH.COM

"Emilie" Cover Art by Gene Sweeney

ISBN 978-0-573-69782-1 Printed in U.S.A. #29238

MUSIC USE NOTE

Licensees are solely responsible for obtaining formal written permission from copyright owners to use copyrighted music in the performance of this play and are strongly cautioned to do so. If no such permission is obtained by the licensee, then the licensee must use only original music that the licensee owns and controls. Licensees are solely responsible and liable for all music clearances and shall indemnify the copyright owners of the play and their licensing agent, Samuel French, Inc., against any costs, expenses, losses and liabilities arising from the use of music by licensees.

IMPORTANT BILLING AND CREDIT REQUIREMENTS

All producers of *EMILIE must* give credit to the Author of the Play in all programs distributed in connection with performances of the Play, and in all instances in which the title of the Play appears for the purposes of advertising, publicizing or otherwise exploiting the Play and/or a production. The name of the Author *must* appear on a separate line on which no other name appears, immediately following the title and *must* appear in size of type not less than fifty percent of the size of the title type.

In addition the following credit *must* be given in all programs and publicity information distributed in association with this piece:

Commissioned and first produced by South Coast Repertory with support from the Elizabeth George Foundation

EMILIE was first produced by the South Coast Repertory in Costa Mesa, California on April 24, 2009. The performance was directed by David Emmes, with sets by Cameron Anderson, costumes by Nephelie Andonyadis, lighting by Lonnie Rafael alcaraz, original music and sound design by Vincent Olivieri, movement direction by Gabriela Estrada, and dramaturgy by Kelly L. Miller. The production stage manager was Jennifer Ellen Butler. The cast was as follows:

EMILIE .... Natacha Roi
VOLTAIRE .... Don Reilly
MADAM .... Susan Denaker
GENTLEMAN .... Matthew Humphreys
SOUBRETTE .... Rebecca Mozo

CHARACTERS

(In order of appearance)

EMILIE DU CHÂTELET – forty, dressed in no particular era, confident and curious

VOLTAIRE (V) – fifty, dressed immaculately in 18th-Century fashion, charming, boyish

PLAYERS

SOUBRETTE – a young woman, mid-twenties, plays **EMILIE** and others:

- **MARY-LOUISE** – simple and stupid
- **DAUGHTER** – direct and strong

GENTLEMAN – a handsome man, thirties, plays **JEAN-FRANÇOIS** and others:

- **JEAN-FRANÇOIS** – young and doting, sincere
- **THE MARQUIS** – serious but warm, very formal
- **MAUPERTUIS** – sexy and academic
- **MARAIN** – snide and proud

MADAM – a slightly older woman, fifties, plays **MOTHER** and others:

- **MOTHER** – serious and wounded
- **MADAM GRAFFIGNY** – obnoxious and rich

A NOTE ON CASTING

The play has been successfully played with 7 actors instead of 5. This requires splitting Gentleman and Soubrette into 2 parts each.

SETTING

A blank theater space. Discovered written on/in this space at the beginning: LOVE, PHILOSOPHY, and F=mv. This is memory - as much or as little set as you want.

Eventually: Centerstage chalkboard, a doorframe, two desks, chairs, and a bed – all of these are mobile. All sets and set-pieces should be reminiscent of a French 18th century aesthetic.

AUTHOR'S NOTES

Tableau – Any choreographed tableau or scene without specific dialogue should be presented with music of the era or in the style of, say, Lully or Rameau

Tally – Emilie will be keeping a tally between LOVE and PHILOSOPHY (far into the 1700's science was known as "natural philosophy")

In Emilie's head

Touch/Presence – Emilie can't touch anyone ever and she can't leave the stage.

Lights – Lights go out when Emilie touches someone – When Emilier-eturns from the blackout, she is always breathless. She goes back to that dark place again, and resurfaces. It shouldn't look pleasant or easy.

Writing – Emilie must also have the capability to write on the walls – chalk or something more inventive. By the end of the play the space should be full.

PRONUNCIATION

Leibniz = *LIE – bnitz*
Marquis = *MAR – KEY*
Cirey = *Sear – EE*
Marquise = *MAR – KEYZ*
Maupertuis = *MAW – pear – TWEE*
Marian = *MAR-AH*
Huygens = *HOW-gens*
Principia = *Prin-KIP-ee-uh*

Not only do the memories serve to represent people in her life, they interact with the narrator Emilie

A BRIEF DEFINITION OF FORCE VIVE and SQUARING

Force Vive ($F=mv^2$) is a scientific concept that was hotly debated in the 17th and 18th centuries. Proposed by Gottfried Leibniz over the period 1676–1689, the theory was controversial as it seemed to oppose the theory ($F=mv$) advocated by Sir Isaac Newton. In Leibniz's view, Newton's equation of was incorrect because it eventually becomes zero, meaning that the force stops and is "dead." Newton explained that God would add more energy to keep the universe going. Leibniz's squaring of velocity meant that force keeps going and doesn't need outside replenishment of energy (i.e. it was "alive"). During the French debates on the subject, Newton's equation became known as "Force Morte," (Dead Force) while Leibniz's equation was called "Force Vive" (Living Force). However, Leibniz's theory was not clearly explicated and lacked a detailed experimental proof, and Newton proved too powerful of an intellectual celebrity to overcome.

By advocating for Leibniz's squaring of Force, Emilie Du Châtelet translated Leibniz's idea in a way that was easily understood and added the decisive evidence on squaring of a Dutch researcher, William 'sGravesande. Today, due in part to Du Châtelet's work, we understand that the two equations are describing different things – Newton's equation describes the Conservation of Momentum ($F=ma$ – Force equal Mass times Acceleration), while Leibniz's equation became what is understood as Kinetic Energy ($E=mv^2$) – Energy equals Mass times Velocity squared).

Scholars see Du Châtelet's legacy as including her advocacy of squaring and her French translation of Newton's Principia. These and her other writings prompted scientists of the following centuries to regard energy as being proportional to mv^2, and she can be traced to Einstein's development of $E=mc^2$.Thank you to Dr. Judith Zinsser, whose mentorship and book, *Emilie Du Chatelet: Daring Genius of the Enlightenment* (Penguin, 2007), gave me so much of the world of this play.

See EmilieLaMarquise.com for more helpful dramaturgy and images for this show.

ACT ONE

(Blackness. Then a single light. **EMILIE** *is in this light. She is a little stunned to be here. She breathes – also stunning.)*

EMILIE. Breath.

(She flexes her hands, testing, getting her bearings.)

Body.
Again.

(She steps out of her spotlight, then steps back in.)

Space.
And Time.
Again?
Life again?
But I'm dead. I'm here. You're here. You're dead? No. Poor logic. Back to facts.

(She starts with the basics…)

There are things called *living* and things called *dead* that exist as people. Hearts and the squaring of hearts.

(She draws a simple heart. Then squares it: ♥^{2}*)*

(She finds **F=mv** *is written.)*

Then there are things called 'living' and things called 'dead' that exist as *Force* and the squaring of Force. Motion, mass. Squared.

(She squares it: **F=mv^2** *remembers this now…)*

Force Vive, it's called. *The Living Force.* "Living" because of that little 2.

(She erases the ^{2}*:* **F=mv***)*

Now it's "dead."

(She squares it again: **F=mv²***)*

EMILIE. *(cont.)* And alive again. Mathematically speaking. But there is something sweeping about this noton: 'when you square it, you give it life.'

(A new energy into…)

I died thinking two things: One – I'm not done. Two?

(She points to the ²*.)*

Two. A number that seems the symbol of a double. But made small and set on high? Is an imperative to expand, extend exponentially – a life-like dynamic – *yes!* Squaring adds *life* – that's why we called it Living Force – that's what I fought for. *That* number in *that* equation was my life's work –
No, my life's *question.* And I died without an answer.
I died thinking: Living and the Living Force…so what?

(She gets it now…)

And that's the impossible question that brought me here:

(She touches the ²*.)*

What do we mean?

(sees that **LOVE** *and* **PHILOSOPHY** *are written)*

And I realize it's a bold attempt to quantify such things…
But Time and Space are generous tonight.
So I ask…
Of all my loving –

(She marks under **LOVE***.)*

and all my knowing –

(She marks under **PHILOSOPHY***.)*

What matters, what lasts? If lasting even matters. What's the point?
Asking tricky questions is what I do best.

EMILIE. *(cont.)* Tonight, I may finally know and finally, finally rest.

(Music and lights flood the space revealing **VOLTAIRE** *and the* **PLAYERS** *in a tableau that would be titled: "Love and Philosophy.")*

My name is Emilie.

(She points to **SOUBRETTE.***)*

I think that one's me, too.

(The trio rushes into another tableau where **VOLTAIRE** *voraciously kisses* **SOUBRETTE.***)*

Definitely me.
Let me see if I can set this stage.

(Points to herself.)

Emilie.

(Points to **SOUBRETTE.***)*

Also me. Somehow.

(Points to **GENTLEMAN.***)*

Perhaps my husband. Or Newton.

(Points to **MADAM.***)*

One of the many courtiers that find me generally intolerable. Or my mother.

(Points to **VOLTAIRE.***)*

And this one. You'll know his name. François-Marie Arouet. Voltaire.

(The tableau shifts into an adoration of **VOLTAIRE**, *the genius.)*

I love this man. And lucky for you we fight in English so you'll be sure not to miss a thing.

*(***EMILIE** *turns to* **VOLTAIRE**, *starts to speak, but the* **PLAYERS** *hand* **EMILIE** *and* **VOLTAIRE** *scripts from which they read right now.)*

VOLTAIRE. "The Life and Love of Emilie La Marquise Du Châtelet." By me. Voltaire.

(turns to her, in character)

"What happened to my life before you? I'd hunted for love, but found only mirages."

EMILIE. *(not "on script")* Wait. Why are we starting here?

VOLTAIRE. A scene in which Voltaire declares his love.

(in character)

"I love you."

EMILIE. *(not "on script")* This isn't the – Start at the beginning.

VOLTAIRE. *(continuing anyway)* "And when love stares you down it is the only thing in the heavens with light."

EMILIE. *(on script)* "Love is science, then."

VOLTAIRE. "Love is *magic.*"

EMILIE. "One should be able to tell the difference."

(off script)

Who wrote this?

VOLTAIRE. *Excuse me.*

EMILIE. *(reads unenthusiastically)* "You distract me, handsome hero."

VOLTAIRE. "A distraction is just an opportunity arising, goddess of the mind."

EMILIE. Goddess of the – ?

VOLTAIRE. "Athena and Aphrodite would bow to your feet –"

EMILIE. *(off script)* Okay – *Stop.* Stop. This isn't right.

(Realizes as she looks at her script)

Because *this* isn't *my* story.

(to **V***)*

This is *yours.*

(She tosses the script. **V** *is insulted.)*

EMILIE. *(cont.)* And tonight is *mine.*

From now on? My story. My life. Because Time and Space have obliged tonight, and they really don't do that very often, and you never know how much of them you're going to get, and I'm *going* to get an answer tonight even if I die trying – *again* – so we need to start at the *beginning,* and start *now*!

(Music – something big)

The scene with the father.

*(**GENTLEMAN** enters, as **EMILIE**'s father.)*

My father was a hero to me. Very simply he allowed me: myself. One of the larger gifts one can be given.

(She marks under **LOVE**.*)*

I learned that he'd loved a woman at court–

*(**SOUBRETTE** enters as this woman.)*

And shunned all others at Versailles to hear her talk about the stars. But. He was a fool, cheated on her with a richer woman, lost her to another man, and cracked his own heart for good.

*(**SOUBRETTE** exits.)*

He married my mother out of convenience – a fact not lost on her.

*(**MADAM** enters as **MOTHER**.)*

My mother sees my education as a waste of time. She thinks my father is rewarding everything she is not.

*(**EMILIE** marks under* **PHILOSOPHY**, *which irritates* **MADAM**, *who exits.)*

*(**SOUBRETTE** enters now as Emilie.* **GENTLEMAN** *leaves.)*

Which is true. I steal my brother's tutor, learn English, Latin, celestial mechanics, all the math there is. My tutors can't keep up.

*(**EMILIE** puts a mark under* **PHILOSOPHY**.*)*

EMILIE. *(cont.)* I host the best minds in France and my husband pays for them. Did I mention I was married? We're skipping ahead.

*(**GENTLEMAN** enters as Marquis Du Châtelet.)*

My husband. A good man. And just. And calm, thank god. I mean the highest compliment when I call ours a true and unique…friendship.

*(**EMILIE** almost marks under love but doesn't. **GENTLEMAN** kisses **SOUBRETTE**'s hand and exits.)*

But he has wars to manage. And I have a name to uphold. And the children. Did I mention I had children? Three. Fascinating creatures raised by the nursemaid which leaves me free to study…

*(**GENTLEMAN**, as Maupertuis, and **SOUBRETTE** study.)*

With my mentor, Maupertuis. The first man outside my family that respects me, challenges me…

(They kiss all over the books.)

An academic relationship. Not without its own distinctive benefits.

*(**SOUBRETTE** stops groping – she's had a thought and abandons **GENTLEMAN** to check her books.)*

*(**GENTLEMAN** is a little perturbed.)*

Maupertuis is my only vein into the heart of academia. I need him, but he doesn't need me.

*(**GENTLEMAN** distances himself from **SOUBRETTE**.)*

As a lady I'm in no position to run out to cafés and mingle with these minds, or god help me, *think out loud…*

*(A doorframe appears. **GENTLEMAN** goes through it.)*

*(**EMILIE** changes **SOUBRETTE** into man's clothes as…)*

EMILIE. *(cont.)* But I want to go where science is *done* – which is not in courts or academies, but in The Café Gradot – an all-male, all-night establishment wherein my sex is restricted to various services unbecoming of my class. And my patience.

So we do what we must.

*(**EMILIE** sends **SOUBRETTE** through the doors.)*

*(**EMILIE** marks under* **PHILOSOPHY**.*)*

Women determine the fate of great nations, of the human race itself, but for us there is no place where we are trained to think, much less to think for ourselves. And if we insist, we are mocked, scorned –

*(Just as **SOUBRETTE** is kicked out again. **SOUBRETTE** exits. **EMILIE** erases the mark under* **PHILOSOPHY.***)*

*(**GENTLEMAN** appears through the door.)*

The men of letters laugh, the men of court frown.

*(**MADAM** appears.)*

And the women…oh they of much gossip and little substance. They are the vipers and hate me because I dare to ask "why" and, more dangerously, "why not?"

But court is essential. So I spend all of my time pleasing those whom I don't even like. I am rich, secure, and…*painfully bored.* And court couldn't care less.

*(**MADAM**, **GENTLEMAN** scoff at her and exit.)*

Then. I meet V. Who cares.

*(Enter **VOLTAIRE**. She underlines the* **v** *in* **F=mv²**.*)*

V for velocity. That sounds about right. Monsieur Velocity.

His reputation hits first. Bard. Bastard. Rebel poet twice locked in the Bastille, always exiled somewhere, and *still* the toast of Paris.

*(**V** sees **EMILIE**, likes what he sees.)*

A chance meeting, but these things are always chance. Until they aren't.

EMILIE. *(cont.)* I see him at a salon discussing Newton, the opera a few times, at court a few more, ballet, gardens, the pâtisserie near my house. It was after we met at Mass that I knew for certain chance had become choice.

The scene at the opera.

(At the opera. Some crackling music/vocals. **VOLTAIRE** *moves to her and they sit. They both know that they're being watched.)*

*(***SOUBRETTE** *joins* **GENTLEMAN, MADAM,** *as audience.)*

VOLTAIRE. Madam Marquise. It is a pleasure to see you. And be seen with you.

EMILIE. We seem to be making a habit of it.

VOLTAIRE. I do love that pâtisserie. How was your éclair?

EMILIE. Much like you I'm afraid: too sweet, not quite filling. How was your tarte?

VOLTAIRE. Couldn't stop myself. Speaking of which, you're not bored by my growing infatuation with you?

EMILIE. On the contrary. I think it's good for your health.

VOLTAIRE. My health? You barely know me, Madam.

EMILIE. I know your reputation. And your work, Monsieur.

VOLTAIRE. You do?

EMILIE. Of course I do.

VOLTAIRE. Of course you do.

EMILIE. Most of your operas by heart. Though I thought that last one was a bit wordy.

VOLTAIRE. Now you tease.

EMILIE. If honesty is game-play.

VOLTAIRE. Everything's a move, my dear.

EMILIE. A dear perhaps, but not yours yet.

VOLTAIRE. I hear a "yet."

EMILIE. And missed the "not."

VOLTAIRE. My god…

EMILIE. You have one?

VOLTAIRE. Only muses.

EMILIE. They're a fickle bunch.

VOLTAIRE. *(falling for her)* Madam, you are…

EMILIE. Speak, poet. The anticipation tortures the air –

VOLTAIRE. *(sincere)* Goddess.
Unstoppable.
I fear –

EMILIE. What's to fear?

VOLTAIRE. A dangerous thing.

EMILIE. For you or me?

VOLTAIRE. We may be in this one together.

EMILIE. You presume too much.

VOLTAIRE. I do.

EMILIE. Well, stop it. I am not that easily deduced.

VOLTAIRE. I *know* that you're a devastating force at cards, you're married to a military creature, and you scare off any allies at court with your excruciating habit of reading.

EMILIE. You're not scared then?

VOLTAIRE. I don't plan on playing you in cards. And don't tell anyone but…I read too.

EMILIE. Well then, perhaps we do have…like minds, mutual interests.

VOLTAIRE. Very mutual, very interesting. And I'm a quick study.

EMILIE. Not too quick – that'd disappoint.

VOLTAIRE. Well, we can discuss your varied preferences over wine tonight?

EMILIE. Monsieur, you're very charming, but you don't get to know my preferences until I know yours. What do you think of Descartes?

VOLTAIRE. A…revolutionary mind.

EMILIE. Leibniz?

VOLTAIRE. Metaphysical mind, unfortunately German.

EMILIE. Newton?

VOLTAIRE. Genius. The world is complete.

EMILIE. And me?

VOLTAIRE. Genius. The world is complete.

*(***EMILIE** *grabs* **V***'s knee suggestively –)*

(Immediately upon their first physical contact, the lights, music, and all breath in the space are gone with a crackle and a spark. Blackness.)

(One light turns on. **EMILIE** *is alone, baffled, scared.)*

EMILIE. I'm sorry. I didn't realize…

(She looks at her hands.)

(With another crackle the lights and music and players return. **VOLTAIRE** *calmly walks to his previous position.)*

VOLTAIRE. Genius. The world is complete.

*(***EMILIE** *goes to touch him –* ***she gets one hand on him and the lights go out more violently****.)*

(One light comes on again. **EMILIE** *is alone, breathless.)*

EMILIE. Descartes was right: mind and body are distinct. In this case profoundly so.
I understand now. No touch.
Touching life is like having it. And I realize that I don't.
This time, my life is not *really* life or mine.
(to God or whoever is in charge:) But I'll take it anyway!

(With another crackle the lights, **V** *and* **PLAYERS** *return.* **EMILIE** *guides* **SOUBRETTE** *to replace her in the scene.)*

EMILIE & SOUBRETTE. And me?

VOLTAIRE. Genius. The world is complete.

*(***SOUBRETTE** *touches* **V** *successfully. The* **PLAYERS** *are scandalized.)*

*(***EMILIE** *marks under* **LOVE**. *Thinks about it. Then marks under* **PHILOSOPHY**, *too.)*

EMILIE. And with a new variable in this glorious equation, the world takes off. Which always makes such a mess.

VOLTAIRE. A scene in which Voltaire woos the unconvinced Marquise.

*(**EMILIE** and **VOLTAIRE**, as well as **GENTLEMAN** and **MADAM**, are playing cards in **EMILIE**'s house. **GENTLEMAN** and **MADAM** eavesdrop avidly.)*

I love you –

EMILIE. My husband is a general–

VOLTAIRE. – in a thousand ways.

EMILIE. – directly under the King.

VOLTAIRE. I'm blushing – I don't blush.

EMILIE. I'm required at Versailles.

VOLTAIRE. When you say 'orbit,' I can't control myself.

EMILIE. Really. Orbit.

VOLTAIRE. God help me.

EMILIE. You're ridiculous.

VOLTAIRE. It's a great way to live. Come away with me.

EMILIE. I can't.

VOLTAIRE. Teach me.

EMILIE. You are a most thrilling wreck but I can't, and you know I can't.

VOLTAIRE. You toy with me. I'm just a puppet to you.

EMILIE. You're a playwright. An *actor.* What can I say?

VOLTAIRE. That you've met your match.

EMILIE. You shouldn't waste your time.

VOLTAIRE. Not a moment wasted with you. Your very breath fuels my *fire.*

EMILIE. That's nice. I win.

*(She wins the card game and takes his money. **GENTLEMAN** and **MADAM** exit.)*

VOLTAIRE. You don't care for me at all.

EMILIE. V.

VOLTAIRE. You'll crush me and I'll die, and you don't care at all.

EMILIE. V.

VOLTAIRE. Yes, Siren?

(He pouts.)

EMILIE. Look at me.

VOLTAIRE. It will set me on fire to do so, but I'll risk it.

EMILIE. I'll explain my hesitation.

VOLTAIRE. Rejection of my noble intentions?

EMILIE. I'm married. What's noble?

VOLTAIRE. They're *sincere* intentions. I can't help it.

EMILIE. That would be your reputation.

VOLTAIRE. I can't help the urge to bite every corner of your frame…

EMILIE. V…

VOLTAIRE. And read every thought in your head…

EMILIE. And if I give you any sign of my true feelings…I'm afraid you'd tackle me.

*(A moment. A smile. Then he tackles her with a kiss. **The lights plunge her into darkness**.)*

(The single light points out **EMILIE**. *She makes another mark under* **LOVE**.*)*

(As the lights crackle back on, we see **VOLTAIRE** *and* **SOUBRETTE**, *as* **EMILIE**, *with much fewer clothes on, grinning, grinning, grinning.)*

(During this, they dress each other, the picture of affection.)

EMILIE & SOUBRETTE. I'd like to have a rule.

VOLTAIRE. A rule?

SOUBRETTE. For you and I. *Just* for you and I.

VOLTAIRE. I'm not good with rules. I find them insistent.

SOUBRETTE. This one's easy. Well. It's simple.

VOLTAIRE. Those are not identical meanings.

SOUBRETTE. One rule.

VOLTAIRE. What simplicity would you have me swear to?

EMILIE & SOUBRETTE. Honesty.

(Pause)

VOLTAIRE. So cruel.

SOUBRETTE. Not punishment. Freedom. Say only what we mean, and mean everything we say.

VOLTAIRE. But…I'm an actor.

SOUBRETTE. To everyone else you are.

VOLTAIRE. We don't have to be honest with everyone else?

SOUBRETTE. God no. We have to survive at court.
But when it's us…love me, mean it, and say it. Or else damn the whole thing.

VOLTAIRE. A daunting experiment.

EMILIE & SOUBRETTE. A worthy one.

VOLTAIRE. You might get hurt.

SOUBRETTE. So might you. All for the deepest kind of knowing.

VOLTAIRE. The deepest kind, the kindest cruelty of the heart and mind –

SOUBRETTE. No poetry. Everyone else gets the show. I get the truth.

EMILIE. The truth.

VOLTAIRE. And that's what we want.

EMILIE & SOUBRETTE. That's what we want.

VOLTAIRE. And we want that badly.

EMILIE & SOUBRETTE. Yes, we do.

VOLTAIRE. Then we'll have it. For you.

SOUBRETTE. And you.

EMILIE. And you.

*(**SOUBRETTE** and **VOLTAIRE** are now dressed, kiss, exit.)*

*(**EMILIE** puts a few marks under **LOVE**.)*

EMILIE. And though tame for a moment, the laws of the heart are based in such violence. They are starved and overwhelmed and just destructive to good behavior. The laws of the universe are clean and *predictable.* To know the universe? Be diligent. To know the heart? Be brave. And so we brave each other – But we're still learning.

*(***VOLTAIRE** *enters with books, upset.)*

VOLTAIRE. I'm a child with all this.

EMILIE. You can't be the best at everything.

VOLTAIRE. Yes I can.

EMILIE. Fine. You know Newton couldn't write a sonnet worth a damn.

VOLTAIRE. You're dismissing this.

EMILIE. You're being a baby.

VOLTAIRE. Kiss me.

EMILIE. V.

VOLTAIRE. Fuck me.

EMILIE. Would you stop. I'm your colleague one minute, then your – what – whore?
Next time you enter a room be kind enough to let me know which way you currently see me.

VOLTAIRE. Currently I see you as…crusty.
I'm going out.

EMILIE. I know the Calculus is hard, and that translation is awful. Just go back to the Latin.

VOLTAIRE. I don't like Latin.

EMILIE. You understand it, V. Just review the equations. On that sheet.

(He goes to the sheet. She doesn't.)

VOLTAIRE. Emilie.

EMILIE. I laid it out for you.

VOLTAIRE. *Emilie.*

EMILIE. I'm writing, V, what?

VOLTAIRE. To whom are you writing??

EMILIE. Maupertuis.

VOLTAIRE. About what?

EMILIE. Orbit of Venus.

VOLTAIRE. Fine.

EMILIE. We have work to do and I'm trying to do it.

VOLTAIRE. With him. Not with me. Just. Fine.

(He starts to walk out.)

EMILIE. V.

VOLTAIRE. I'm ill.

EMILIE. You're not ill.

VOLTAIRE. Felt it all week.

EMILIE. You're frustrated, not sick.

VOLTAIRE. Don't bother.

EMILIE. Are you jealous that I'm sharing orbits with another man.

VOLTAIRE. Do not mock me, woman. You'll have plenty of time to write to your younger, meatier friends about all the things I'm too daft to understand, when I die from being sick. Which I am. At least I'll get a statue.

(pause)

EMILIE. Sit.

(He nearly "faints." **MADAM** *enters.)*

Some very hot tea and lemon. Warm towels.

MADAM. Is he all right?

EMILIE. Oh, I think he'll pull through.

MADAM. *(with complete lack of verve)* Saints be praised.

*(***MADAM** *leaves.* **V** *smiles and tries to kiss her.)*

EMILIE. Too sick for math, too sick for that.

*(***V** *settles.* **EMILIE** *picks up a book. In her own though*

VOLTAIRE. I just forget that you care. And that I c you care. It's quite insidious this cycle we're need time.

EMILIE. *(thinking out loud re: her book)* Time and space are absolute.

VOLTAIRE. I can't force you to love me.

EMILIE. But force is not, in Newton's equation.

VOLTAIRE. But you really should.

EMILIE. Newton *multiplies* speed by mass – so all force eventually cancels out – so there's *no more* energy.

VOLTAIRE. I'm so tired.

EMILIE. So the cosmos stops.

VOLTAIRE. You wear me out.

EMILIE. Which *isn't true.*

VOLTAIRE. It's true!

EMILIE. So Newton thinks *God* intervenes just to keep us going?

That's ridiculous.

VOLTAIRE. And I know it's ridiculous for a celebrity to admit, but I *need* you.

EMILIE. God doesn't need to *intervene* – why bother making the cosmos if you have to keep it *tuned.*

Leibniz wrote about this – *Force Vive.* Energy that's not a *multiple* of speed, but speed *squared* – which means energy is exponential – which means it doesn't run out which means God doesn't need to wind us up!

tices that she's not listening.)

alk about myself for one minute…

ks to the F=mv².*)*

d's in the squaring.

were doing Calculus.

ted.

what?

.)

re that

n. I just

EMILIE. The universe!

VOLTAIRE. I don't care about the universe if you don't love me!

Just say you do so I can rest.

(She gestures for **SOUBRETTE** *to take over.)*

EMILIE & SOUBRETTE. I love you!

EMILIE. Now shut up so I can think.

*(***V** *grabs* **SOUBRETTE** *[as Emilie] into a hug.)*

*(***EMILIE** *marks under* **LOVE** *and* **PHILOSOPHY***.)*

EMILIE. And I start to think that both love and energy are surprisingly exponential. It would be easier to rest, to release, to stop like Newton's equation expects us to. But even complicated love doesn't give up that easily…

*(***GENTLEMAN** *appears as The Marquis Du Châtelet, Emilie's husband.)*

GENTLEMAN. *(to us, not entirely sincere about this…)* The scene in which Emilie's husband returns and is…happy for her.

(He bows, she courtesies, they stand as friends.)

You're happy then?

EMILIE. I am. Are you? I never ask that.

GENTLEMAN. Property, children, the king's favor. A wife I'm proud of. That's a good life by all accounts.

EMILIE. And you look so handsome. Wars aren't all that bad are they? You're fooling all of us ladies with all that talk of battles and bravery.

GENTLEMAN. Of course not. Very serious. The campaign –

EMILIE. A joke, dear. Joking.

GENTLEMAN. Oh. Well.

You look – healthy. I mean lovely. Sturdy, well-fed.

EMILIE. You're making me feel a bit bovine, dear, but thank you.

GENTLEMAN. Sorry. Soldier talk.

EMILIE. Which doesn't require much flattery, I see.

GENTLEMAN. Yes. No. Well.

The children are growing up into willful creatures like their mother.

EMILIE. And kind like their father. Gabrielle is pretty enough. I think she'll marry well.

GENTLEMAN. I'll certainly see to that. And Florent is proving his skill in military language?

EMILIE. And mathematics. He could be a scholar.

GENTLEMAN. Doesn't have it in him.

EMILIE. If he kept studying he could be something.

GENTLEMAN. He may have your mind, but he's got my name. That makes him a general. Stop the tutor at sixteen. I'll take it from there.

EMILIE. As you see fit.

(Small pause)

GENTLEMAN. Will Voltaire be joining us at the opera tonight?

EMILIE. Seeing as how he wrote it, I expect he'll be there.

(Small pause)

GENTLEMAN. Is he…treating you well?

EMILIE. He's good…for me. Not like your kind of good. You are the earth, he's more of the…elements. Thunder and lightning and…well.

GENTLEMAN. I'm glad you're sufficiently captivated. I know you're hard to entertain.

EMILIE. I am not. I'm quite agreeable. With decent books. And competent card players. And – you're right, I must be exhausting.

GENTLEMAN. You are. I miss it.

EMILIE. Thank you, dear.

(They don't know what to say. **SOUBRETTE** *[as Emilie] enters replacing her again.)*

GENTLEMAN. Off we go?

EMILIE & SOUBRETTE. Off we go.

*(**GENTLEMAN** takes **SOUBRETTE**'s arm and exits. **EMILIE** watches him go. Turns to us.)*

EMILIE. This is where it gets confusing, because *that*'s Love too.

*(She makes another mark under **LOVE**.)*

Not the fire kind, but the *bread* kind, the comfort kind. We have nothing in common but our offspring, but he is a *good* man and he loves me. Quietly and sure.

*(She makes another mark under **LOVE**.)*

And it's ludicrous that safety bores us so.

*(**VOLTAIRE** enters in a flurry.)*

VOLTAIRE. *(to us)* The scene in which Voltaire is almost imprisoned in the Bastille…again.

*(to **EMILIE**, rushed)*

They're on their way. Here to arrest me. Right now.

EMILIE. What did you do?

VOLTAIRE. The markedly brilliant letters I wrote praising the English. The king is mad that I'm so stunningly *right*, that he wants me killed. Which is so French, that the irony is completely lost on him.

EMILIE. You weren't supposed to publish those.

VOLTAIRE. *They* weren't supposed to. The printers! I hate printers.

EMILIE. You can't humiliate a king like that.

VOLTAIRE. I hate kings.

EMILIE. All of Paris is probably reading it.

VOLTAIRE. And I really hate Paris.

EMILIE. You love Paris when it loves you. You *knew* you were playing with fire. Stop playing with fire! Don't you learn?

VOLTAIRE. Only makes me smarter.

EMILIE. Where will you go?

VOLTAIRE. I don't know.

EMILIE. They're coming *now* and you don't *know*?!

VOLTAIRE. Come with me.

EMILIE. Come with you *where?*

VOLTAIRE. ANYWHERE. NOT here! Come!

EMILIE. No!

VOLTAIRE. Now!

EMILIE. GO, V! Before you can't. GO now GO!

VOLTAIRE. And so I go. Not knowing when I'll see you again. I go.

EMILIE. *Wait.* Wait. I have a chateau in Cirey. A family estate. It's a wreck. Barely habitable.

VOLTAIRE. Still waiting for how this helps me.

EMILIE. You'd be safe there.

VOLTAIRE. And you'd be there? I want you there. I need you there.

EMILIE. Stop wooing. I can't think.

VOLTAIRE. Your resident poet? Harmless, literary.

EMILIE. My husband could be convinced.

VOLTAIRE. I'll pay anything.

EMILIE. That might help.

VOLTAIRE. And you'll come?

EMILIE. I don't know.

VOLTAIRE. You're coming.

EMILIE. *They're* coming! You GO!

VOLTAIRE. Say you'll come!

EMILIE. I won't SAY anything to you EVER AGAIN – Which is what happens when you go to the Bastille!

VOLTAIRE. Meet me at Cirey.

EMILIE. GO.

VOLTAIRE. Come.

EMILIE. NOW!

(He goes, comes back for a passionate kiss. But she ducks his advance just in time to avoid another black-out. **VOLTAIRE** *continues offstage.)*

EMILIE. The scene in which he tries every method of roping me in…to my *own* house.

*(**VOLTAIRE** appears. These are their letters.)*

VOLTAIRE. Dearest Emilie, I am safe at your chateau. Thank you. It's a dump. Come to me.

EMILIE. I am a lady of stature. I can't.

VOLTAIRE. Did I mention that you are my heart beating? Also, your husband likes me and/or my money. Come.

EMILIE. I can't run off to the country.

VOLTAIRE. The renovations are majestic!

EMILIE. How will I work? The books I need.

VOLTAIRE. I know all the booksellers.

EMILIE. The equipment I need.

VOLTAIRE. I've already had it shipped.

EMILIE. The spine of the thinking elite is here –

VOLTAIRE. We'll invite them.

EMILIE. – and the court –

VOLTAIRE. Not them.

EMILIE. – and the gossip if I left, my daughter's suitors, my family name, and – and the world doesn't work like that!

VOLTAIRE. That's why we make our own. Love and Philosophy await.

(Beat)

EMILIE. You are an irritating man. I'm on my way.

VOLTAIRE. You are?

EMILIE. It seems I love you desperately.

VOLTAIRE. Desperation can be quite enjoyable. Be my muse.

EMILIE. If you'll be mine.

VOLTAIRE. Genius. The world is…

EMILIE & VOLTAIRE. Complete.

(She breathes and turns to us.)

EMILIE. The moment I leave Paris to live in the country and *study*...with *him?* That's when I switch from eccentric to rebel over night.

*(**EMILIE** walks to **VOLTAIRE**, who turns to her.)*

The scene in which I come home.

*(They are at Cirey – and it's abuzz! The **PLAYERS** are busy servants in the house.)*

VOLTAIRE. Now. The house is in a good state. The grounds are fertile, the orchards ripe, and the peasants pleased. I've stocked the stables, imported an Italian gardener and garden, and built a new wing.

EMILIE. A new wing?

VOLTAIRE. Everything painted as you like.

EMILIE. Blue and yellow?

VOLTAIRE. Green and white. We'll adjust.

*(**MADAM**, as a servant, runs off with these new orders.)*

My room is connected to yours, as is the library.

EMILIE. I brought a carriage-full of books.

VOLTAIRE. I brought three.

EMILIE. Luxury!

VOLTAIRE. And I threw in a chapel for good measure.

EMILIE. Can't hurt.

VOLTAIRE. The entire East wing is for experiments, and I've already sent for a barrage of tools and measures.

EMILIE. Air pump?

VOLTAIRE. Yes.

EMILIE. Thermometers?

VOLTAIRE. Of course.

EMILIE. Calibrated Vacuum Bell.

VOLTAIRE. I'll find out what that is then make sure it's on the next shipment.

EMILIE. This is a kingdom.

VOLTAIRE. Ready for a queen.

EMILIE. My king?

VOLTAIRE. Jester at best.

EMILIE. You are not that humble.

VOLTAIRE. Then King it is.

EMILIE. And your plays? You can't perform in the hallways. Where will you work?

VOLTAIRE. I'm glad you asked. With full permission from your generous husband to transform his attic, I present...

(He reveals a small stage where the unprepared servants are in some happy tableau.)

Le Petit Theatre.

EMILIE. V...

VOLTAIRE. Isn't it charming?

EMILIE. It's perfect.

VOLTAIRE. I'll write, you'll star, we'll grab servants for the bit parts.

EMILIE. It's Paris without Parisians.

(The servants relax the tableau – back to drudgery.)

VOLTAIRE. You like it?

EMILIE. Yes.

VOLTAIRE. You're happy?

EMILIE. Yes.

VOLTAIRE. And you think you have a chance of staying that way?

EMILIE. Yes.

VOLTAIRE. Then. Queen of the House, Lady of the Library, may I acquaint you with the intimate details of my personal chamber. There are a few things that need a thorough going over...and over...

*(**EMILIE** gestures to **SOUBRETTE**, who enters and replaces **EMILIE**, as **VOLTAIRE** carries her off.)*

EMILIE. This place is not of the world.

*(**EMILIE** makes a few marks under **LOVE** and **PHILOSOPHY**.)*

*(The servants [**GENTLEMAN** and **MADAM**] get to work arranging and hauling books and equipment into the space. **EMILIE** supervises.)*

We build the perfect home, laboratory, palace, circus…

*(**V** emerges with fresh pages of a new opera. Guides **SOUBRETTE**, [as Emilie], to the stage, snatches **GENTLEMAN** from work and starts directing them.)*

We build the largest library in Europe…and live in it.

*(**V** and **SOUBRETTE** read books, trade books, write, and ramble – their desks face each other. **GENTLEMAN** tries to enter with a message but instead becomes a shelf for all the books they use which they pile on top of him.)*

The best minds in science and art fight for a seat at our table.

*(Soon **GENTLEMAN** has so many books in his arms that he is unable to see…**V** places a final book to cover **GENTLEMAN**'s eyes so that he can successfully smooch **SOUBRETTE** [as Emilie]. The smooching takes **V** and **SOUBRETTE** off, as **GENTLEMAN** leaves with the books.)*

And for the first time in my life I think that happiness may not be *having* all the answers…it may be having time and space to wonder.

*(**V** enters buttoning up some piece of clothing, snatching a book from **GENTLEMAN** as he passes. **EMILIE** and **V** study separately.)*

EMILIE. I wonder…You wouldn't want…?

(She stops herself, which stops him.)

VOLTAIRE. Want what?

EMILIE. Nothing. Ridiculous thought.

VOLTAIRE. I tend to like those. What?

EMILIE. No no no. I was in someone else's life for a moment.

VOLTAIRE. What were you thinking?

EMILIE. No.

VOLTAIRE. What what what?

EMILIE. A baby. A baby.

(Pause)

VOLTAIRE. What kind?

EMILIE. Of baby? With me.

(Pause)

VOLTAIRE. Oh. Why?

EMILIE. Progeny, V. In general.

There's a reason I didn't actually ask you.

VOLTAIRE. I think you just did.

EMILIE. You pressed me.

VOLTAIRE. I did not. You were bursting.

*(**V** is now giggling.)*

EMILIE. I was in the middle of my retraction. Stop it. I was trying to – stop laughing. It was a thought experiment. Not a real thought.

And I know it's impossible. I couldn't pull off legitimacy with my husband at war. The rumors would be mortifying, and the theatrics to fool the neighbors – it'd be Olympic.

VOLTAIRE. You thought this through.

EMILIE. Well…yes. I thought, and to my credit quickly *re*thought with much better judgment, that if we were to do such a ridiculous thing, it would be…generally unstoppable.

*(**V** is quiet. **EMILIE** picks up his mood.)*

VOLTAIRE. But…our progeny is thought and theatre.

EMILIE. It is.

*(**V** sees her disappointment. Time for a gift. He claps his hands and the **PLAYERS** rush into a tableau. **MADAM** presents **EMILIE** with a brand new book.)*

VOLTAIRE. Goddess. Because I cannot think without you. Because our legacy is built in books…I present this engraving for the front piece of my new book – *The Elements of Newton* – which without your consummate help I would have had neither the knowledge nor patience to complete.

*(A tableau of Newton, see Appendix 1. Newton [***GENTLEMAN***], Emilie [***SOUBRETTE***], and* **VOLTAIRE** *[himself].* **V** *shows* **EMILIE** *his creation.)*

*(***V** *takes his place in the tableau.)*

Newton shines the light to you, who then reflects it to me. I am the scribe of your dictation. And the world will know it.

EMILIE. V…It's gorgeous.

VOLTAIRE. It's you. And it's true. You gave me the world.

EMILIE. *(turned on by all this)* Well you better give it back. Now.
Upstairs.

VOLTAIRE. And ye shall receive.

(The tableau disbands as **V** *and* **EMILIE** *can't wait.* **MADAM**, *as Madame Graffigny, enters. She is stuffy and rude, but always smiling.)*

MADAM. Good evening.

VOLTAIRE. *(not pleased)* It used to be.

EMILIE. Madame Graffigny. I hope you're enjoying your stay with us.

MADAM. Oh, we're all talking again. How nice.

EMILIE. I'm sorry?

MADAM. I think it's fine manners to lock yourselves up all day talking about planets, while your guest wanders this place alone. I didn't get my café till noon.

VOLTAIRE. The height of misfortune.

MADAM. And the post is so slow I haven't gotten any of my letters.

VOLTAIRE. Travesties abound.

MADAM. And though the food is marvelous –

VOLTAIRE. Triumph!

MADAM. I can't stand eating by myself. A lady of my stature deserves –

VOLTAIRE. A nice long walk?

MADAM. Monsieur.

VOLTAIRE. A horse ride, far away?

MADAM. Good god.

VOLTAIRE. A part in my opera. That's it.

MADAM. Oh, no. I can't sing.

VOLTAIRE. Then you'll defy our expectations.

(**GENTLEMAN** *enters with the post.*)

I'll send up the script, rehearsals tonight, and you must, *must* go practice your lines.

(**VOLTAIRE** *takes the mail from* **GENTLEMAN** *and shoves him toward* **MADAM. V** *reads a letter.*)

(**MADAM** *is escorted off by* **GENTLEMAN**.)

EMILIE. You *have* a new opera?

VOLTAIRE. There're not that hard to come by. Upstairs?

EMILIE. What's that?

(**VOLTAIRE** *shows her the letter.*)

VOLTAIRE. The Academy posted a contest. Upstairs?

EMILIE. A contest?

VOLTAIRE. Which we can discuss later.

EMILIE. *(reading the letter)* A prize from the Academy of Science on the nature and propagation of fire…
We'll submit.

VOLTAIRE. Of course we will.

EMILIE. Real collaboration, V.

VOLTAIRE. So very real.

EMILIE. Joint study!

VOLTAIRE. Works for me.

EMILIE. An alliance of our best ideas, working together –

VOLTAIRE. I don't really care what we're calling it now, I'd just like to get on with it.

EMILIE. Missed your window. Now...the nature of fire.
What are the basic questions?
Fire at its essence is…a substance itself? Or a reaction?

VOLTAIRE. Fire is made of…

EMILIE. Light, obviously.

VOLTAIRE. Heat, of course. Mass? Weight?

EMILIE. Can we weigh fire?

VOLTAIRE. We must.

EMILIE. We'll test it.

VOLTAIRE. Measure it.

EMILIE. In order to prove –

VOLTAIRE. What shall we prove?

EMILIE. Whatever we find to be true. Through *experiment.*

VOLTAIRE. Through experiment.

EMILIE. We'll need lots of metal.

VOLTAIRE. Weigh it, melt it, weigh it again.

EMILIE. And keep meticulous records.

VOLTAIRE. Meticulous.

EMILIE. And we could be the first people ever to calculate the weight of fire!

VOLTAIRE. I'll start with the dedication. Something somber but uplifting, I'm thinking couplets.

EMILIE. V.

VOLTAIRE. Prose?

EMILIE. We don't have anything to dedicate. First we work, then we…art.

VOLTAIRE. Right.

EMILIE. Right.

VOLTAIRE. Fire.

EMILIE. Fire.

VOLTAIRE. An essay on the nature and propagation of fire by Voltaire and La Marquise…

*(**MADAM**, as Graffigny, enters with a theatrical mask.)*

MADAM. For the opera!

VOLTAIRE. Play's canceled.

*(***V*** exits.* **MADAM** *storms off.)*

EMILIE. *(to us)* We spend all night, every night setting things ablaze. And though gorgeous and warm for a moment…there's a reason you don't play with this stuff.

It's not going as planned so he's bending the data. The experiments are lazy, the results are unclear, and he's seeing only what he wants to see. That's not science, that's drama.

(A breath)

The scene in which I tell him he's wrong. Also drama.

*(***V*** enters with notes.)*

EMILIE. It doesn't work, V.

VOLTAIRE. Yes it does. Of course it does.

EMILIE. When we melted lead there was no weight change. When we melted iron it was heavier than when we started. There's no consistency.

VOLTAIRE. We already know what we're looking for. It's just bad equipment.

EMILIE. Then it's bad work. We have to redo it.

VOLTAIRE. Start over?

EMILIE. Start over.

VOLTAIRE. Because our equipment fails us?

EMILIE. Because our premise is wrong.

VOLTAIRE. It's Newton's premise.

EMILIE. Then Newton is wrong.

VOLTAIRE. He can't be wrong.

EMILIE. Fire is *not* material. It has no weight. Newton is wrong.

VOLTAIRE. When did you decide this? We are supposed to be collaborating.

EMILIE. Then listen to me. Read Leibniz.

VOLTAIRE. I'm not using that German. Newton is the pinnacle of our age, and if he says fire has weight then it has, and I'm going to prove it.

EMILIE. And if Newton was looking at our data he'd agree with me. I won't submit that.

VOLTAIRE. Then you won't.

EMILIE. Good. I've been drafting other ideas and –

VOLTAIRE. *I'll* submit it.

(She stops.)

EMILIE. Oh, V. Don't.

VOLTAIRE. I've worked on it for months, the deadline is in two weeks. I'll submit it. With credit to you, of course.

EMILIE. I don't want credit for that.

VOLTAIRE. I'm not starting over.

EMILIE. The method is wrong. The results are, therefore and without a doubt, *wrong.*

VOLTAIRE. I can come to my own conclusions.

EMILIE. For *once* just consider the idea that you *could* be mistaken, that you *could* be fallible in this *one* scenario, lonely as it may be in the immensity of your usual correctness. Science isn't theatre, you can't pick the ending because it sounds nice. Listen to me.

VOLTAIRE. Listen to *me.* You think The Academy would ever *ever* give this prize to a woman? If you want to do this work you've got to do it with me. You're nothing to them. A rich courtier with no reputation except as a card shark and a…tramp. Who are they going to validate, you or me? A saloniste or a –

EMILIE. A minstrel? A hypochondriac sycophant? They don't care about you either. They humor you. They manage you. Stick to fiction.

VOLTAIRE. Admit to fact.

EMILIE. You first.

VOLTAIRE. You really won't submit?

EMILIE. Most certainly not.

VOLTAIRE. Then we've come to an impasse.

EMILIE. Most certainly.

(Pause)

VOLTAIRE. Fine. What are you going to do?

EMILIE. Oh, you know. Practice cards and, what was it, tramping?

VOLTAIRE. As a favor, as an amicable gesture showing no bitterness between friends and colleagues, I can give you a mention in my dedication. For your work.

EMILIE. Please, *please,* don't bother.

VOLTAIRE. You could use the recognition.

EMILIE. And you could use a failure. *Goodnight.*

(Pause. **V** *moves away, preparing to speak to us.* **EMILIE** *nods to* **SOUBRETTE** *who begins writing as Emilie.)*

And so without a plan, enough time, or a moment's hesitation, I begin to write. All night, every night, by myself, just a candle and a quill, and soon I learn the biggest lesson of my life…that a candle and a quill is all I'll ever need.

EMILIE & SOUBRETTE. Certainly all I can ever count on.

*(***V** *turns to us and presents his paper loudly.)*

VOLTAIRE. An Essay on Fire by Me. Voltaire.
"As I have proven, Newton explains that fire is mass…"

*(***EMILIE** *turns to us, quietly at first.)*

EMILIE. "Fire is not mass. It has no weight, therefore does not – *cannot* – respond to gravity."

VOLTAIRE. "Fire *does* respond to gravity just not…obviously."

EMILIE. "Anyone can see that a candle's flame stays tall even as it goes out. Fire is the very opposite of gravity."

VOLTAIRE. "As for Light and Heat…"

EMILIE. "Fire *is* Light and Heat, is friction, is reaction, is…
A hint at the invisible breath of life that God scattered on his work without which the Universe could not subsist a moment more."

VOLTAIRE. "That's for my *next* essay."

*(***V** *gathers his work carefully into an envelope and hands the package to* **GENTLEMAN** *[a postman].*

*(***V** *remains onstage, confident, obstinate, unaware.)*

*(***SOUBRETTE** *hands* **GENTLEMAN** *her essay. He exits with both pieces of mail.* **SOUBRETTE** *exits.)*

*(***EMILIE** *marks under* **PHILOSOPHY** *and looks at* **V***.)*

EMILIE. And I start to see what he can't: that he may not be my true half. And then I think…perhaps no one is. Or worse, perhaps someone is and I'll never know whom. And that's a cold thought. And, as we've discussed, he tends to escort a certain heat. So I forgive him over and over again. Like Newton's God resetting the planets. An imperfect equation…that works for now.

*(***GENTLEMAN** *enters with a letter, hands it to* **V***.)*

VOLTAIRE. The Academy's announced the winner.

EMILIE. The winner? Who is it? Who won?

VOLTAIRE. I did.

(She's disappointed.)

And you.

(She's stunned, thrilled.)

VOLTAIRE. *(cont.)* Actually some hack took the top prize. But it seems that *we both* received honorable mentions. *'We'* being the new concept here.

(Pause)

When did you write it?

EMILIE. Nights. Till sunrise.

VOLTAIRE. Alone?

EMILIE. Yes.

VOLTAIRE. Experiment?

EMILIE. Candles.

VOLTAIRE. Who knew?

EMILIE. The maid.

VOLTAIRE. The maid and not me.

*(***MADAM***, as the maid, leaves quickly.)*

VOLTAIRE. What was your thesis?

EMILIE. Theoretical. Light and heat are related, might be the same.

VOLTAIRE. Light and heat are the same?

EMILIE. Don't be angry. I spared us a fight.

VOLTAIRE. Then let's not argue. We're both right…or wrong. I can't tell anymore.

Now will you please explain your theory, or must I wait and read it like everyone else.

EMILIE. Read it like what?

(She grabs the letter from him. Reads.)

VOLTAIRE. They'll publish us both.

EMILIE. Mine too? The Academy will publish *mine*?

VOLTAIRE. I convinced them to print *all* the honored essays along with the winning bit of futility. I didn't know it would be such a direct favor, but…

*(***SOUBRETTE*** runs on as Emilie to hug ***V*** very sincerely, no sex in this hug, just friendship.)*

EMILIE & SOUBRETTE. Thank you.

*(***SOUBRETTE*** exits.)*

VOLTAIRE. I didn't do much.

EMILIE. You did. For your own benefit, granted, but in the end it was quite generous.

VOLTAIRE. You deserve it. You're a stunning woman. And an impressive man.

*(***V*** exits. ***EMILIE*** turns to us.)*

EMILIE. I take the compliment. Then think, why is manliness the compliment? The mind, the earth, the stars, all of the things I care about are sexless.

And those sexless secrets of the cosmos only come to those who fight to know. I fight. And it's the *fighting* that's the compliment.

Then I ponder my daughter. Who does not fight.

(**SOUBRETTE** *enters as Gabrielle, Emilie's daughter. Young but regal.*)

EMILIE. *(cont.)* She is all woman, and will have a much easier life for it. She is loyal, demure, and…entertainable. She is marrying a prince today.

The scene in which –

SOUBRETTE. The scene in which the daughter is seen and finally heard. On her wedding day.

SOUBRETTE. I wanted to be like you. I still do.

EMILIE. No you don't. Your life will be much better than mine. Marrying royalty makes you –

SOUBRETTE. Just another wife.

EMILIE. It makes you queen. And everyone wants to be queen.

SOUBRETTE. Everyone wants to *choose* to be queen. Why don't I get a choice?

EMILIE. Because you don't need one.

SOUBRETTE. You got one.

EMILIE. I'm an exception. And being exceptional is exhausting. You don't want that.

SOUBRETTE. How do you know?

EMILIE. Didn't those nuns teach you to respect your mother?

SOUBRETTE. My mother is a picture in my locket. I don't know you. You shipped me off to a convent. Now you marry me off to a prince. I don't have a mother, and I don't have a life that's mine, and that's your fault.

EMILIE. My *fault* that you have a future? You should be grateful that your father and I *arranged* for such a –

SOUBRETTE. *Bargained.* You bargained *me* for such a life.

EMILIE. Gabrielle, there are so many other girls who would've begged –

SOUBRETTE. But I'm not other girls. I'm your girl. Your girl.

EMILIE. And that makes you lucky. So live your lucky life. It will be easier, by far –

SOUBRETTE. You keep saying *easier.* I don't want easier. You didn't care what was easy. You wanted what you wanted, and you gave me up for it.

EMILIE. I didn't. I didn't give you up.

SOUBRETTE. You chose books over me. I want a choice. *Your* choice.

EMILIE. You don't want –

SOUBRETTE. *I do.*

EMILIE. You don't want my life.

SOUBRETTE. You never gave –

EMILIE. You want an easy life.

SOUBRETTE. Never gave me –

EMILIE. A good life.

SOUBRETTE. A chance. You got one. And you could've given me mine. Instead. You gave me what every other *kept* woman gives her stupid daughter. Instead of what you know, here's what I know…

(**SOUBRETTE** *changes her tone.)*

SOUBRETTE. A girl does not slouch. Does not speak in excess. Does not question or laugh loudly. She marries rich. She obeys. She submits. And she–

EMILIE. I'm sorry.

SOUBRETTE. She has –

EMILIE. I'm sorry.

SOUBRETTE. And she has an easy life. Good luck with yours.

(**SOUBRETTE** *starts to leave, then comes back for a harsh hug.* ***The lights crackle and plummet out to blackness****.)*

(Immediately the lights rise. **SOUBRETTE** *is gone.* **EMILIE** *is alone.)*

EMILIE. And I see what I missed: myself in her. What have I done? What any thoughtless *man* would do. I assumed and missed a woman of my own…element.

I'm sorry. I am so sorry.

(Nothing.)

EMILIE. *(cont.)* What do I do? What can I give her to give her a chance? Everything I know? A book. Foundations of science for anyone – The whole universe – for all, for her.

(Regroup)

The scene in which I write my first book. The silent scene that takes back the world. For my daughter. Force Vive, Space Time, fire and life, and love and – this is it – this is purpose, progeny, *living force.*

(A writing desk and chair appear.)

(She looks at us.)

This could take a while.

(She claps and the house lights turn on. She shoos us into…)

End of Act

INTERMISSION

(During the intermission **EMILIE** *writes and writes. She never leaves the stage – or appears not to. She stretches, paces, works out an equation or two. Perhaps* **MADAM** *brings her some water.)*

(As the intermission ends **EMILIE** *is satisfied with her work. As the house lights dim and Act Two begins,* **EMILIE** *gently closes the cover to her finished book and waits for us to sit…)*

ACT TWO

EMILIE. The scene in which the book is done, printed, read all over France, then all over Europe.

(V enters with Emilie's book.)

VOLTAIRE. The scene in which a science text, *by a woman,* captivates the thinking world.

*(***GENTLEMAN***, as Mairan, enters reading Emilie's book.)*

EMILIE. And the world…

*(***MADAM*** and ***SOUBRETTE***, as Emilie's daughter, enter reading the book as well.)*

…finally realizes with whom they are dealing.

(reading the cover)

Foundations of Physics

By La Marquise

"The study of physics is made for all of us. And it's the key to all discoveries. Never stop learning."

*(The ***PLAYERS*** read from Emilie's book.)*

SOUBRETTE. "Our most sacred duty is to give our children an education that prevents them from regretting their youth."

*(***EMILIE*** flips to a later chapter, as do the ***PLAYERS***.)*

MADAM. "Because we can *all* rise to the truth, like those giants who climbed up to the skies by standing on shoulders. Leibniz learned from Huygens. Newton from Kepler."

*(***EMILIE*** flips to a later chapter, as do the ***PLAYERS***.)*

EMILIE. "But sometimes truth is snuffed out by bombast. Like the essay by Monsieur Mairan, current secretary of the Academy, denouncing *force vive* with unfounded proofs."

VOLTAIRE. *Emilie…*

(V tries to stop her from saying this last bit, but…)

EMILIE. "He is a course in how *not* to proceed through your studies."

VOLTAIRE. That's a mistake.

EMILIE. What?

VOLTAIRE. That last part? You just insulted the secretary of the Academy.

EMILIE. He's an idiot.

VOLTAIRE. And the *secretary* of the Academy.

EMILIE. Then he'll understand it's just friendly critical discourse.

(As **EMILIE** *goes to put a mark under* **PHILOSOPHY**…**GENTLEMAN**, *still as Mairan and quite upset, turns.)*

GENTLEMAN. Madam Marquise,

Though you somehow found yourself published on the topic of Force Vive, you rush to judgment like any woman confronted with ideas beyond her skill. My dear, you simply did not understand my mathematics, nor did you properly read my own writing as you misquote me throughout. I would be happy to guide you through my reasoning, if you would permit me at your little Leibniz academy in the fields. But as my equations prove there is no need to square force: Newton is right, Leibniz is wrong, and you, my dear, are out of your element. All you need to do, Madam, is to read, and reread, and perhaps you could bring us something worth our time.

(A moment for his own satisfaction)

EMILIE. *(to us)* It is an honor just to merit a response. But I'll break him anyway.

EMILIE & MADAM. Response to Secretary Mairan, from La Marquise.

MADAM. *(like reading juicy tabloid)* "I am sorry to play the mother to your wandering child, but it is, after all, the instinct of my sex to correct a failure in order to educate."

EMILIE. I have been waiting for this chance.

MADAM. "On the point of my misquoting your work. I have included a table listing exact references, so you can stop misquoting *me.*"

EMILIE. A public battle…

MADAM. "And I attached complete solutions to all aforementioned problems. I can walk you through the difficult bits."

EMILIE. That I can win in my sleep.

MADAM. "Force Vive is the only theory that explains the Dutch experiments on velocity. So I suggest that *you* keep reading for you've obviously got some catching up to do. Yours humbly…"

*(**GENTLEMAN** is outraged and starts to speak –)*

EMILIE. *(to **GENTLEMAN**)* I win.

MADAM. "La Marquise."

*(**MADAM** yanks the book from **GENTLEMAN**.)*

*(**EMILIE** makes a solid mark under **PHILOSOPHY**. **MADAM**, **SOUBRETTE**, and **GENTLEMAN** leave.)*

EMILIE. I think I won.

VOLTAIRE. You did.

EMILIE. I did? I did.

VOLTAIRE. And everyone will know.

EMILIE. This is what it feels like. Glory.

(She does some cheer for herself.)

*(**V** starts to leave.)*

EMILIE. Where are you going?

VOLTAIRE. Work to do.

EMILIE. Celebrate! This is a major battle won. A victory! Progeny, V.

VOLTAIRE. Not mine.

*(**V** leaves. To us…)*

EMILIE. An odd thing when triumph over rivals matches the jealousy of friends. But, I am not apologizing. I know who I am.

Damn the heart; long live the mind.

*(**EMILIE** marks under* **PHILOSOPHY**.*)*

And it seems we damned them both. Cirey is quiet now – no dinner debates, or even dinners. Our fire is fading. So we both grow colder and colder alone.

*(**MADAM** brings **EMILIE** a pamphlet. **V** enters.)*

V?

VOLTAIRE. Yes.

EMILIE. Did you send a letter to the Academy refuting my book?

VOLTAIRE. Yes.

EMILIE. Did you know that they published it? This letter dismissing Force Vive. You wrote that about me and then published it?

VOLTAIRE. I did.

EMILIE. And you don't tell me?

VOLTAIRE. I thought that's what we did; submit in private and surprise each other.

EMILIE. You attack my work, my competence?

VOLTAIRE. You rejected Newton; that's irresponsible.

EMILIE. I haven't rejected Newton. It's inquiry. I'm studying.

VOLTAIRE. You publicly adopt this Leibniz absurdity. Force Vive is a joke, it's nonsense. That little 2 is presumptive and overreaching and –

EMILIE. Oh you're squaring *me* now?

VOLTAIRE. I have to defend the truth! They respect my opinion.

EMILIE. I gave you your opinion.

VOLTAIRE. And then turned your back on it.

EMILIE. On *you.* It's not the little 2, it's not Newton, it's *you* I've betrayed, correct?

VOLTAIRE. This isn't ego, it's fact. My ideas match the entire continent's.

EMILIE. Which makes you popular not right! You're as bad as the monarchy – anyone who doesn't agree with you should be skewered.

VOLTAIRE. Leibniz is incorrect, and what's worse, *obviously* so.

EMILIE. Newton squares distance in the force of gravity – why not square velocity in Force Vive?

VOLTAIRE. Because gravity isn't energy!

EMILIE. You oversimplified the argument.

VOLTAIRE. You've chosen a ridiculous argument!

EMILIE. You wouldn't know if it was or not!

VOLTAIRE. You can't prove Force Vive!

EMILIE. *I already did* – but *still* you fire off your mouth to impress some Academy dogs, and make *me* sound like a –

VOLTAIRE. What? Like a stubborn *woman*?

EMILIE. Like a poet dressed up as a scholar.

(Beat)

You may want to change the dedication in your next book. I wouldn't want people to mistake us for equals or friends.

VOLTAIRE. All this for a little 2.

EMILIE. All this for truth, you jackass. No man can know all.

VOLTAIRE. But a woman can?

EMILIE. Next time, let me know when you trash my work in public. I'd be happy to correct your manuscript. You misspelled "Leibniz." *Twelve times.*

(Pause. **EMILIE** *starts to leave.)*

VOLTAIRE. I have something to say.

EMILIE. Put it in a novel.

VOLTAIRE. I can't have sex anymore.

(Pause)

I'm old. Sick. Near death. I don't want to disappoint.

EMILIE. "Disappoint." Don't flatter.

VOLTAIRE. I just wanted to inform you of the malfunction of my…machine.

EMILIE. Good thing we are very much past fucking as delicacy.

VOLTAIRE. You don't need me for *anything* then.

EMILIE. Stop acting like a wounded cat – you betrayed *me*!

VOLTAIRE. You betrayed me first! Leibniz is a betrayal of everything I stand for!

EMILIE. Then stand up to this. You want Newton? I'll translate.

VOLTAIRE. What are you talking about?!

EMILIE. *The Principia.* The whole of it.

VOLTAIRE. Whose translation?

EMILIE. *Mine.*

VOLTAIRE. You aren't.

EMILIE. I am.

VOLTAIRE. Since when?

EMILIE. About ten seconds ago.

VOLTAIRE. Translating?

EMILIE. And *revising.*

(This stings **V.***)*

There are bits that need it.

VOLTAIRE. What bits?!

EMILIE. Force Vive.

VOLTAIRE. WHAT.

EMILIE. Force Vive belongs in Newton's universe and I'm gonna put it there.

VOLTAIRE. You can't just DO that!

EMILIE. I'll work on the cosmos; you focus on your pants.

VOLTAIRE. Don't throw that around. I don't deserve that.

EMILIE. What do you deserve then, a dirge for your manliness? *I* deserve better than this. I deserve more than this insult to everything I was for you.

VOLTAIRE. Emilie.

EMILIE. If I'm so awful, so useless to you, say it so I hear you say it, so we can be *done*!

(Pause)

VOLTAIRE. It seems we are growing apart.

EMILIE. That'd be the trend.

VOLTAIRE. I'm sorry.

EMILIE. Of course you are.

VOLTAIRE. I care for you deeply.

EMILIE. Of course you do.

VOLTAIRE. And I always will.

EMILIE. But for now? For now, nothing, V. You give me nothing.

*(***V*** takes the cue and leaves.* **EMILIE** *attempts to be calm.)*

And *nothing,* as a concept, is a larger conversation than one would think. Nothing is a definition of everything. How do we *feel* nothing? And why does absence weigh so heavy on the heart?

(Stopping her emotions)

EMILIE. No. That's not the point.

The point is…that I just committed to translate the most important book in the modern world to prove I'm right…and piss him off.

(She breathes.)

Give me Newton!

*(***GENTLEMAN*** enters as* **NEWTON** *with trepidation – these are big shoes to fill. He hands her a large notebook,* The Principia.*)*

EMILIE. *Philosophiae Naturalis Principia Mathematica.*

(re: the book in her hands)

Newton's Laws. And once you understand them, you can understand *almost* everything. And though he and I disagree on a few minor points, Newton is the most complete understanding of the cosmos created by a human mind. But Force Vive belongs in his cosmos too…and I'm going to put it there.

*(**EMILIE** opens the book.)*

And so I translate from his Latin:

Newton's Laws of Motion.

*(**SOUBRETTE** enters, she is not Emilie, but someone new and cute.)*

*(**VOLTAIRE** enters and sets **SOUBRETTE** moving/dancing – all an exhibition of the following laws…)*

One. That all bodies persist in the same state of rest or uniform motion in a straight line.

*(**VOLTAIRE** contacts **SOUBRETTE** in some way that changes her trajectory/dance.)*

Two. That change in movement is always proportional to and in the direction of force.

*(**SOUBRETTE** and **VOLTAIRE** dance together dropping a letter as they spin.)*

EMILIE. *(cont.)* Three. That action and reaction are always equal & opposite.

*(**EMILIE** sees the letter, picks it up, and reads)*

"My dearest uncle."

*(At this **SOUBRETTE** and **VOLTAIRE** stop. They are caught. **SOUBRETTE** reads the letter too, all smiles.)*

EMILIE & SOUBRETTE. "You flatter me beyond compare. I can't wait to be in your arms again. As always, my ass is yours."

EMILIE. Her ass is – ?

VOLTAIRE. Oh dear.

EMILIE. Shall I go on?

VOLTAIRE. I know the rest.

EMILIE. I'll just catch up.

EMILIE & SOUBRETTE. "When last you wrote me, I was given over to those special shivers"

VOLTAIRE. Emilie.

EMILIE. I swear to God if you don't let me finish, I will castrate you right here.

VOLTAIRE. Continue.

SOUBRETTE. "That only a lover can impart. I long for you, dear uncle."

EMILIE & SOUBRETTE. "Let the gossips be damned. Yours in all love,"

SOUBRETTE. Marie-Louise.

EMILIE. Your niece Marie-Louise? Your niece.

VOLTAIRE. That sounds worse than it is.

EMILIE. I'm so glad your machine's working again. It just took the right greasing.

VOLTAIRE. I am capable of explaining if you'd let me.

EMILIE. Explain.

(Pause)

VOLTAIRE. I am a man.

EMILIE. Better be more than that.

VOLTAIRE. I don't need an excuse! I don't need to be excused. I don't need permission. I don't need to be judged by you.

EMILIE. Because nothing matters that's not directly related to you.

VOLTAIRE. Oh god.

EMILIE. Or your reputation

VOLTAIRE. Fine.

EMILIE. Or your little ass, you stupid, awful man.

VOLTAIRE. I'm sorry you found that.

EMILIE. You're sorry I found *out*?

VOLTAIRE. I was going to tell you.

EMILIE. Oh well, thank you for being such a gentleman.

VOLTAIRE. For everything I did for myself, that I *needed* for myself, I'm sorry. I'm sorry I ruined *your* version of how *my* life would happen. I'm sorry!

EMILIE. You betray me, in my own house, twice?! You trash my work, you lie to me, you ruin everything we built, everything that mattered, wrecked it, ripped it up, ripped it, ravaged it – everything that made sense – GONE!

(She realized she has just ripped Newton's Principia, *pages scatter on the floor.)*

VOLTAIRE. I just…forgot that you care –

EMILIE. *Stop talking.*

*(***EMILIE** *whistles to* **MADAM** *who charges* **V** *and slaps him hard.* **MADAM** *nods to* **EMILIE** *and leaves.)*

I would suggest, if you wish to retain my friendship and the immediate privileges that arrangement entails, not least of which is keeping you out of jail on an alarming number of occasions, that you refrain from any form of literary bribery until I am quite out of range. You have betrayed me and broken my heart. Get the hell out of my house.

*(***VOLTAIRE** *leaves. A moment to pick up the pages, salvage the precious book.)*

*(***EMILIE** *wipes through all the marks under* **LOVE** *– as well as the* ^{2} *of the* ♥*.)*

EMILIE. One must study throughout.

*(***VOLTAIRE** *and* **SOUBRETTE***, as Marie-Louise, enter and she lets him have his way.)*

*(***EMILIE** *senses their behavior but won't acknowledge them.)*

Study not only affords women a chance at the glory denied them in so many other pursuits –

(They knock something over, challenging Emilie's focus as Emilie make a few marks under **PHILOSOPHY***.)*

EMILIE. – but you study *alone.* And who else do you have? Candles and quills and…Newton.

*(**GENTLEMAN** as Newton enters, not sure if this was his cue or not. It's not. He exits apologetically.* ***EMILIE*** *tries to continue with forced confidence.)*

A scene in which Emilie translates three major proofs of the essential laws of attraction as presented by Sir Isaac Newton. Alone.

*(**VOLTAIRE** and **SOUBRETTE** face each other.)*

One. Gravity affects the shape of the earth, flattening at its poles.

*(**VOLTAIRE** and **SOUBRETTE** lean out creating a dome with their outstretched arms. They are a flattened globe.)*

Two. The three-body problem. Or how the gravity of every object in the same system affects every other.

*(**VOLTAIRE** [the Earth] and **SOUBRETTE** [the Moon] start orbiting and revolving. They make **EMILIE** the Sun.)*

Three. The behavior of comets.

*(**SOUBRETTE** is now a comet who soars by **EMILIE** – not amused.)*

No matter how long their tenure in the depths of space. Gravity brings them back. Always.

*(**EMILIE** is left alone as **VOLTAIRE** and **SOUBRETTE** go.)*

But "always" is not as comforting as it once was.

(pause)

We are a mess of trajectories. Tangled and unfeeling. And I wish I could unfeel.
I'm smarter than this. This shouldn't be so hard.

*(**MADAM** enters as Emilie's mother.)*

And then I think of my mother. A safe, exacting woman, who had an easier life for it. And I think…is easy so bad?

MADAM. The scene with the mother.

EMILIE. These rules will make you happy, she'd say.

MADAM. A girl does not slouch, does not speak in excess, or laugh loudly attracting negative attention. Do not look your betters in the eye. Do not read in public.

EMILIE. How do I *know* when I'm happy? I'd say.

MADAM. Take a man's right arm, not left.

EMILIE. Are you happy?

MADAM. When introduced to him, smile, bow, and repeat his name. In that order.

EMILIE. Happiness be easier to remember.

MADAM. Do not take cheese at dinner parties. Powder your wig persistently. Display your bust enthusiastically. Be demure.

EMILIE. Then I'm happy?

MADAM. Do not *question.* Comment, only.

EMILIE. Fine. This is not *real.*

MADAM. This is how things are.

EMILIE. This is artifice. Rules for sitting, rules for eating, rules for talking, rules for *not* talking, rules for hair, for hands, for shoes, for fans.

MADAM. The proper technique of fanning! Hold away from one's face, snap the wrist, raise the arm, and flap like a bird.

EMILIE. So I play peacock?

MADAM. Emilie.

EMILIE. You just said!

MADAM. You'll never marry.

EMILIE. Then I can stop all this.

MADAM. The *mouth* should be kept closed when…*thinking.*

EMILIE. Why?!

MADAM. No questions!

EMILIE. But the world is bigger than this!

MADAM. Not for you. So follow the damn rules.
It's easier. And *easy* makes us happy.

*(**MADAM** exits.)*

(**EMILIE** *turns to us, furious.)*

EMILIE. *But it doesn't.* Easy is ignorance, is a myth. That the greatest thinkers were ever remotely, even for a second *satisfied,* is mythology. Newton was not content, he was ravenous, he was wracked, he was *not done,* and I'm sure he was furious on his deathbed because of it.

Because the only thing that lasts – the only thing that you can count on to be there for you? Not people, not love…Physics.

That's the only thing that works like God is supposed to: Fair and constant.

Let's move on.

(Pause. Nothing happens.)

Please?

(Nothing.)

EMILIE. *(cont.)* The scene in which Emilie gets a break? Or a friend?

(**V** *approaches her cautiously. She sighs, to us…)*

Of course, physics often promotes *circular* behavior… here I go again.

VOLTAIRE. Marquise. It's been too, too long. Months without a word…

EMILIE. *(totally lying)* Has it been? Hadn't noticed. So busy with the Newton.

VOLTAIRE. *(trying to apologize sincerely)* Yes. Well. Emilie. I came here to – to tell you – to *ask* you if you could – *we* could…*have* each other again.

EMILIE. Oh, V, I'm done with "having."

VOLTAIRE. I don't mean – I mean that I need you. Extensively. And I know that I was, on occasion in the past, unthinking.

But I'm broken open, empty without you. You are my... buoyancy. Without you I sink.

EMILIE. You sank yourself.

VOLTAIRE. I know I did. And it wrecked me. Please. Take me back.

EMILIE. The world can't go back, it'd be rude if *we* did.

VOLTAIRE. Then forward. As friends.

EMILIE. *(scoffs)* Friends?

VOLTAIRE. *Eventual* friends?

(beat)

Because you love me.

(She glares.)

Eventually?

(Beat)

EMILIE. The Marquis and I have been invited to Luneville.

VOLTAIRE. Luneville? Ugh. Dreadful place –

EMILIE. The Duke's a fan of your work.

VOLTAIRE. – with surprisingly good taste.

EMILIE. My husband will come later, but you're welcome to join me. If you won't be a pain.

VOLTAIRE. I suppose I could summon up my best behavior.

EMILIE. That won't be any fun.

VOLTAIRE. There's my girl.

EMILIE. Not yours. But glad you're back.

(to us)

And part of me thinks that Physics has some heart after all.

*(**VOLTAIRE** smiles, ushers her into…)*

The scene at a new court, with old friends made new.

*(The royal court of Luneville. **MADAM**, **SOUBRETTE**, **GENTLEMAN** [as Saint-Lambert], create a tableau of the court.)*

*(**VOLTAIRE** and **EMILIE** are greeted with applause and they each are separated for conversation – **EMILIE** with **SOUBRETTE** and **MADAM**; and **VOLTAIRE** with **GENTLEMAN**.)*

MADAM. It is very special of you to join us, Marquise.

SOUBRETTE. We've all heard of you, it's true.

EMILIE. We're so honored to be here.

GENTLEMAN. The court is complete with its geniuses. We're thrilled to have you.

VOLTAIRE. Glad to know I'm still able to thrill someone.

MADAM. I hear you're very skilled, Madame.

SOUBRETTE. In the arts of natural philosophy?

EMILIE. It is both habit and passion.

GENTLEMAN. It won't be long before the Duke will demand a play. You are the best in the country.

VOLTAIRE. The country?

GENTLEMAN. The world surely.

MADAM. I couldn't help but notice your carriage.

SOUBRETTE. Full of books?

EMILIE. I'm working while visiting, yes.

MADAM. And your husband?

EMILIE. Still called to the front. Excuse me…

*(**EMILIE** notices **GENTLEMAN**, trying to overhear…)*

GENTLEMAN. I'm a poet myself. And it would be the pride of my days were you to peruse my work at some point in your tenure.

VOLTAIRE. And you are?

GENTLEMAN. Jean-François de Saint-Lambert. Poet, soldier. At your service.

VOLTAIRE. Well. Good to have you floating around.

*(**EMILIE** and **GENTLEMAN** finally lock eyes.)*

GENTLEMAN. *(to **EMILIE**)* The scene when we meet.	**EMILIE.** *(to **GENTLEMAN**)* The scene when we meet.

VOLTAIRE. Soldier-Poet, have you met La Marquise du Châtelet?

GENTLEMAN. Madame Marquise, it is a rare honor to meet you.

EMILIE. My pleasure.

VOLTAIRE. He's a poet, Emilie.

EMILIE. I heard.

GENTLEMAN. A poet only humbly.

EMILIE. I haven't met a humble poet yet.

VOLTAIRE. She's talking about me.

GENTLEMAN. If I may say, your work elucidating the great thinkers of our age is a monument to your sex and country.

EMILIE. Sex and country? My goodness.

GENTLEMAN. I've read your books.

EMILIE. Have you?

GENTLEMAN. *Foundations of Physics.* Enlightening.

VOLTAIRE. That'd be the point.

EMILIE. I'm glad you enjoyed it.

GENTLEMAN. More than enjoy, Marquise. To see a clear review of Leibniz's philosophies, and your amazing argument for Force Vive. The squaring of force –

VOLTAIRE. Oh god.

GENTLEMAN. – was a revelation to me. Time and space and…all that.

EMILIE. Time and space?

VOLTAIRE. Time and space.

EMILIE. Well.

GENTLEMAN. Well.

VOLTAIRE. *Well.* He liked the book, Emilie.

EMILIE. He did.

GENTLEMAN. Your beauty was also mentioned, though not nearly well enough detailed. I am quite–

VOLTAIRE. Let me guess. Speechless?

GENTLEMAN. On the contrary, I feel the need to express. To write. You instantly inspire.

(to **V***)*

I'm sure you've experienced a similar urge to compose, Monsieur.

VOLTAIRE. A *real* urge? It must be literature.

EMILIE. He's had a long trip. Excuse his entire nature.

GENTLEMAN. Genius should never be excused.

EMILIE. But it could be pleasant.

VOLTAIRE. Why don't we go rest, Emilie.

GENTLEMAN. Certainly I'm sure I'm exhausting. I should have quieted my–

VOLTAIRE. Urge?

GENTLEMAN. Please forgive. I've overwhelmed the already fatigued.

EMILIE. Oh, I'm not tired. In fact, I think I'd like to hear your work?

GENTLEMAN. You would?

VOLTAIRE. You would?

EMILIE. I'll need some company before my husband arrives, and I love poetry.

VOLTAIRE. She's talking about me.

EMILIE. No I'm not.

*(***SOUBRETTE** *replaces* **EMILIE** *again.)*

EMILIE & SOUBRETTE. Indulge me, Monsieur.

*(***SOUBRETTE** *takes* **GENTLEMAN***'s arm.* **MADAM** *and* **V** *exit.)*

EMILIE. And like the most natural thing in the world…we begin.

Not many words work to explain it.

*(***SOUBRETTE***, as Emilie, and* **GENTLEMAN** *walk and talk together.)*

Force.

*(***SOUBRETTE** *points to the sky explaining the stars.)*

Acting on Mass.

*(***SOUBRETTE** *rushes to him, a very clear kiss.)*

Acting on each other. Everything on everything. Love, again, anew, *all* new, and almost – dare I say it, with apologies to my mother – *easy.*

*(***V** *walks on, interrupting the kiss.* **SOUBRETTE** *and* **GENTLEMAN** *break apart and* **EMILIE** *takes over as* **SOUBRETTE** *steps aside.)*

VOLTAIRE. How's the book coming?

EMILIE. Excellent. How's the play?

VOLTAIRE. Marvelous.

EMILIE. Good.

VOLTAIRE. I just love it here.
Don't you just love it, Monsieur?

GENTLEMAN. Oh. Yes. Quite.

VOLTAIRE. Good boy. Heel.

EMILIE. Coming to cards?

VOLTAIRE. I look forward to losing.

EMILIE. Maybe you'll get lucky.

VOLTAIRE. Maybe I will.
The Duke calls you, boy. Wouldn't dally.

(V exits.)

GENTLEMAN. I adore you.

EMILIE. I can tell.

GENTLEMAN. This is the most astonishing –

EMILIE. Astounding –

GENTLEMAN. Complete surprise.

EMILIE. I didn't expect.

GENTLEMAN. I can't resist.

EMILIE. I hope you don't.

GENTLEMAN. Everyday.

EMILIE. Yes.

GENTLEMAN. Forever.

EMILIE. God yes.

GENTLEMAN. You are…You are…

EMILIE. Speak, soldier-poet.

GENTLEMAN. The surprise of my life. The hope of my heart.

*(**SOUBRETTE** runs on and takes **EMILIE**'s place as they kiss. **GENTLEMAN** and **SOUBRETTE** exits.)*

*(**EMILIE** makes many marks under **LOVE**.)*

EMILIE. There must be a trigger in women that sways us to forget the bruises of certain activities like childbirth, men, and other dangerous sports. It's either madness or martyrdom or…hope.

*(**V** enters.)*

VOLTAIRE. I've decided that I'm happy.

EMILIE. Glad to hear it.

VOLTAIRE. For you.

EMILIE. Oh. Thank you.

VOLTAIRE. You love him?

EMILIE. I do. V, he's effortless. Passionate and gentle, and his poetry's not bad at all, and he makes me want to…

*(She jumps in place. **V** cackles.)*

You think I'm a fool.

VOLTAIRE. Gave that up a while ago. But you knew that.

EMILIE. I'm glad we're friends, V. It'd be a shame to waste all that history.

VOLTAIRE. My favorite alchemy is the process by which happy hindsight turns tragedy into comedy.

EMILIE. Alchemy's not good science. But you knew that.

VOLTAIRE. Knowing better never really worked for me.

EMILIE. I recall. You are hard to forget.

VOLTAIRE. That was the general intention.

Don't let this boy distract you. You've got work to do.

*(**V** jumps, exits.)*

*(**GENTLEMAN**, [as Saint-Lambert], returns.)*

EMILIE. I thought the Duke –?

GENTLEMAN. The Duke can wait. I love you. I said, *adore.* But I meant love. Love is what I meant. *Mean.* Now I don't know what you think, but I think you think like I think, and I think we're fated for each other and without a doubt completely and utterly in –

*(She kisses him hard and true. **The lights go off with a huge crack.**)*

(A spot comes on. **EMILIE** *is alone, and remains there waiting for the lights to return.)*

(One light comes on. In it **SOUBRETTE** *and* **GENTLEMAN** *are moving together sweetly. This may be sex or dancing. But it's calm.* **EMILIE** *watches.)*

EMILIE. "Love" is an overused term. Ours is like air and water: pure, clear, and known to move mountains. This is it. Happy mind. Happy heart. Thank you god… and your best equations.

(The lights still aren't on all the way.)

But too much of anything, even the best things, can overwhelm.

(She starts to put a mark under **LOVE** *but stops…)*

*(***SOUBRETTE** *looks at* **GENTLEMAN***, touches her stomach, worried.* **GENTLEMAN** *realizes.)*

EMILIE & SOUBRETTE. The surprise of my life. The hope of my heart.

*(***GENTLEMAN** *escorts* **SOUBRETTE** *offstage.)*

*(***V** *enters, as does a card table.* **EMILIE** *sits and plays.)*

EMILIE. The scene in which…

(To **V***.)*

I'm pregnant.

*(***V** *stops.)*

VOLTAIRE. Are you sure?

EMILIE. It's always a bit of a mystery, but all facts point to it.

VOLTAIRE. And the boy knows?

EMILIE. He's not a boy, and yes, he knows.

VOLTAIRE. And the spouse?

EMILIE. These things happen.

VOLTAIRE. "These things happen?"

EMILIE. I need you. You can't be angry.

VOLTAIRE. *I'm not angry, I'm horrified.*

*(***V** *throws his cards on the table.)*

EMILIE. I'm too old.

VOLTAIRE. Quite possibly.

EMILIE. It's not a good time.

VOLTAIRE. I agree.

EMILIE. Younger than me have died.

VOLTAIRE. *(bursting) Yes, they have.*

(Pause. A supportive tone.)

I'm sorry.

EMILIE. Help.

VOLTAIRE. I'm sorry.

EMILIE. I have to finish the Newton.

VOLTAIRE. You have nothing to worry about.

EMILIE. Every moment I should be working.

VOLTAIRE. You'll be fine.

EMILIE. The calculations are good.

VOLTAIRE. You are the picture of health.

EMILIE. The illustrations need work.

VOLTAIRE. You'll be fine.

EMILIE. I'll be fine.

VOLTAIRE. You can't –

EMILIE. *(scared now)* I really can.

VOLTAIRE. The world would stop.

EMILIE. It wouldn't blink.

VOLTAIRE. The sun would fade.

EMILIE. Shine on and on.

VOLTAIRE. This is not how…Emilie…

(Beat. Locked into each other. Breath. They both gain composure. Tonal shift.)

VOLTAIRE. I think we should categorize this child under your miscellaneous works. You are so multitalented.

(She laughs. She goes to touch his hand but the lights hiss at her. She stops.)

EMILIE. This child could be…like me.

VOLTAIRE. Two of you…I wouldn't want to miss that.

EMILIE. I'll need some of our equipment from Cirey. For the Newton.

VOLTAIRE. Why do you need equipment if you're translating?

EMILIE. Because I've almost figured out how Force Vive works *with* Newton, and if I can do *that*? That's real.

VOLTAIRE. Isaac be damned.

EMILIE. Isaac would be proud. Now will you help me or continue being an ass?

VOLTAIRE. Although I so enjoy being an ass, as you know, I will, of course, help in any way Madame Marquise.

EMILIE. V. I won't leave till it's done.

VOLTAIRE. *(a compliment)* Then I hope it confounds you forever. Though that's unlikely.

*(**V** goes to exit, but stops. He doesn't hear this…)*

EMILIE. We speak so well. Tight sentences delivered with confidence. And I wish that I could tell you what I actually mean. I am not this presentable inside. I've got no etiquette. I scream and cry. I don't want words anymore. No use. Just be. Simple be.

*(**V** exits. **EMILIE** makes a mark under **LOVE**. **GENTLEMAN**, as Saint-Lambert, enters.)*

And you. New and true love. You are easiest to me, thank god. For us I wish a real chance…

*(**EMILIE** makes a mark under **LOVE** as **GENTLEMAN** changes into her husband – or into his memory.)*

EMILIE. And you. Husband. Constant enthusiast. I wish you could know how much I honor you. And that I'm sorry for this.

*(**GENTLEMAN** exits. **EMILIE** makes a mark under **LOVE**.)*

I'm sorry. I'm sorry.

(Beat. She is alone. No one's coming on.)

Sorry, and running out of time, and no closer to knowing anything new.

(giving up)

So *STOP.* Just stop. We don't have to go on anymore. I understand.

(Emilie's desk returns, two huge books as well – one is Newton's Principia *and one is hers for writing.)*

I said I understand. I don't want to do the rest.

*(***SOUBRETTE** *enters carefully.)*

I know what happens! And I want to stop!

(pause)

WHY NOT?!

*(***SOUBRETTE** *turns to her.)*

SOUBRETTE. Incomplete.

EMILIE. I don't care.

*(***MADAM** *enters.)*

SOUBRETTE. Time and space –

EMILIE. Are on my side tonight. So tell them to quit this. It's over. I'm done.

MADAM. Incomplete, Emilie.

EMILIE. I know the end of this story. Completed, thank you.

MADAM. Time and space –

EMILIE. *Yes.* They've been very kind, but I don't want any more.

MADAM. You don't decide.

EMILIE. It's my life! Who else decides!?

MADAM. Time.

SOUBRETTE. And Space.

EMILIE. Well I know this story, and I don't care for this last bit, so let me go.

MADAM. You can't go.

SOUBRETTE. You have to finish.

EMILIE. Then do the rest without me.

(**EMILIE** *starts to leave.)*

SOUBRETTE. Emilie!

MADAM. No!

(**V** *and* **GENTLEMAN** *run on stopping her.)*

GENTLEMAN. *Wait.*

VOLTAIRE. You can't.

EMILIE. Can't what?

GENTLEMAN. Exit.

EMILIE. Why not? What's out there?

MADAM. Nothing.

SOUBRETTE. Real Nothing.

GENTLEMAN. All this is for you, Emilie.

VOLTAIRE. All you.

SOUBRETTE. And you're not done.

MADAM. You're not.

SOUBRETTE. You can't be.

MADAM. Because.

SOUBRETTE. You're not complete.

MADAM. That question of yours?

SOUBRETTE. Unmet.

MADAM. Your story?

SOUBRETTE. Untold.

GENTLEMAN. So finish this. If you don't, all the nothing wins.

EMILIE. But, I don't know what it means.

GENTLEMAN. Because stories aren't equations.

VOLTAIRE. Lives aren't either.

SOUBRETTE. They don't have solutions.

EMILIE. Then why am I here? I need answers!

MADAM. Answers aren't always the truth.

EMILIE. I don't understand.

GENTLEMAN. Maybe you will.

MADAM. If you get to the end.

(pause)

SOUBRETTE. Let me.

*(***MADAM*** gestures to* **EMILIE** *to sit, which she does.* **SOUBRETTE***, [as Emilie], gets into place.)*

I rise at eight and work till three. Café from three to four, and resume work. Stop at ten to eat alone.

*(***V*** walks to her.)*

Talk with V till midnight.

*(***V*** exits.)*

Resume work till 5.

*(***GENTLEMAN*** walks with her, reading to her.)*

Walk with Jean-François every day. A new poem every morning.

(He exits. **V** *walks to her with a book.)*

Work until V brings me news and books.

(He exits. **GENTLEMAN***, [as the Marquis], enters.)*

Dinner with my husband. More work.

*(***GENTLEMAN*** exits.)*

Because above everything. I must risk all for all and do this work. This work is…

EMILIE. All.

SOUBRETTE. This work is –

EMILIE. Mine.

SOUBRETTE. This work is –

EMILIE. Me.

*(***SOUBRETTE*** nods to* **EMILIE***, then exits.)*

(Beat. Eureka…)

Because *lives aren't equations*…they are variables *inside* them.

The governing equations are universal,

but a life lived fully can still change the universe.

I can still change the…

*(***EMILIE*** squares to the equation:* $F=mv^2$*)*

EMILIE. *(cont.)* Force Vive – The Living Force – Life's there – *I'm* in there.

*(**SOUBRETTE** crosses the stage very pregnant helped by **GENTLEMAN**.)*

Wait wait – No –I know what's coming and I know its coming fast but – I have to know what all this means!

*(**SOUBRETTE** contracts, moans – They exit as)*

Not yet. I'm close. More time. Give me time!

*(**EMILIE** fills the walls with Force Vive equations…)*

Time. Space. WHERE'S THE ANSWER?

*(**SOUBRETTE** wails from offstage – **MADAM** comes running…this baby is on its way.)*

The scene with the book and the baby.

*(**V** runs across the stage as **SOUBRETTE,** offstage, screams and the baby is born.)*

(A bed enters.)

*(**MADAM** crosses with the swaddled infant as **SOUBRETTE** is led onstage to the bed by **GENTLEMAN**, **V**.)*

*(**GENTLEMAN** kisses her forehead.)*

Not yet. No…

*(**V** kisses her forehead, hands her a book. **V** exits with **GENTLEMAN**.)*

I don't understand yet. Slow down – I'm not – I'm *not* –

*(**SOUBRETTE** closes the books.)*

SOUBRETTE. Done.

EMILIE. *NOT DONE.* There's *more.*

SOUBRETTE. Done.

EMILIE. "Done" isn't an answer.

You said I'd understand. And I don't. And I'm dying. *And – Where's my answer*?!

*(The **PLAYERS** and **V** appear. Very quiet at first.)*

MADAM. We thought you'd like to know…

GENTLEMAN. Jean-François is devastated. Never thinks of another like you.

VOLTAIRE. V eulogizes you well. And often. "Half his soul," he says.

MADAM. And means.

GENTLEMAN. Husband never marries again. Wouldn't know how or whom.

MADAM. The baby girl dies in a year. Laid with you in tomb, poor thing.

GENTLEMAN. There's a revolution you'll be glad you missed.

MADAM. But the book survives.

EMILIE. It does?

VOLTAIRE. So does that little 2.

EMILIE. What about it?

GENTLEMAN. The work, the woman lives hundreds of years on.

MADAM. And becomes the work of hundreds after you.

VOLTAIRE. Progeny, Emilie.

EMILIE. What kind?

GENTLEMAN. Legacy, Emilie.

EMILIE. *What kind?*

MADAM. Complete, Emilie.

EMILIE. *NoNo, NOT* complete. NOT enough. I'm NOT DONE!

(But the **GENTLEMAN**, **MADAM** *and* **V** *are gone –)*

I died thinking that the first time, and *I'm not doing it again.*

*(***EMILIE** *fills the walls with Force Vive equations.)*

Time and space have obliged tonight – They have obliged ME tonight – *It is MY time and MY space* – and equations – and Living Force and Force of Living and…

(She looks at **F=mv²***.)*

EMILIE. *(cont.)* Force of…

Because when you square it…you *give it life…*

(Looks at **SOUBRETTE***…)*

Or life gives you
A day out of dark;
The chance *(*or two*)*
To make your…

(She marks the **F** *into an* **E** *– it reads* **E=mv²**. *Smiles)*

And I don't even know what that means…

(The revelation…she turns to us…)

But *you* do.
And *that's* my answer.
Not *what* we mean, but *that* we mean.

(Beat. Full, changed beat. **EMILIE** *and* **SOUBRETTE**, *the two of them, connect.)*

EMILIE & SOUBRETTE. Done.

(A brave beat. She's ready.)

EMILIE. The scene in which I die.
But not yet.

*(***EMILIE** *grabs* **SOUBRETTE***'s hand – The lights crack and wail –)*

NOT YET.

(The lights do not go out –)

The scene I never got. The scene that no one does. The scene when *I* hold my hand – when I *am* all I need – because in this scene? Nothing gives me meaning but me.

(A moment between the **EMILIES**. *Bittersweet but strong. To* **SOUBRETTE** *– only for* **SOUBRETTE***.)*

This is it.
The weight of the world. The knowing and the not.

And for all your knowing, you are blessed with more –
Questions. Love and so many questions.
And all the answers may not come –
But the asking makes us last –
And that makes you right *and wrong*, done and *never* done –
And that's the point, Emilie.
That's it.
This is it.
Thank god....
And your best equations.

(**EMILIE** *holds* **SOUBRETTE** *tight as* **SOUBRETTE** *dies –*
The lights rise into flaring white, then plunge out.)

(One light on **EMILIE, SOUBRETTE** *is gone. Beat.*
The light is going out again, and so is she...
She knows this is her last speech.
She is precise with it, in awe of it, ready...)

All we have is the moment of having.
And the hope that we knew something real.
All we have is the meaning of having,
All we have is the force and the life
This moment, this having –
And this.
And this.
And...

(Breath. Blackout.)

End of Play

APPENDIX 1

Front Illustration of Voltaire's *Elémens de la philosophie de Neuton* (Amsterdam, 1738). Newton (upper left), Emilie (upper right), and Voltaire (bottom left).

OTHER TITLES AVAILABLE FROM SAMUEL FRENCH

NIGHT SKY

Susan Yankowitz

Drama / 3m, 3f / Unit Set

This extraordinary drama premiered to acclaim in a New York production directed by Joseph Chaikin and starring Joan MacIntosh. It was subsequently produced Off-Broadway in a revised version directed by Daniella Topol and featuring Jordan Baker in the central role.

Night Sky theatrically explores what Steven Hawking has called the two mysteries remaining to us: the brain and the cosmos. When she is hit by a car, the brilliant and articulate astronomer Anna loses her ability to speak, a condition known as aphasia. What emerges from her mouth is a hodge-podge of unconnected words alternately confusing, funny, original and wise – and sometimes all four. In a series of brief, often comic episodes, the play follows Anna through her illness and ultimate acceptance of herself – a personal triumph, despite a continuing infirmity – and dramatizes the impact of her changed circumstances on her lover, her teen-aged daughter, and her professional life.

Everyone will be touched by the themes this play considers – language, inner and outer space, the challenges of a devastating affliction, the consolations and ordeals of family life and, most of all, the universal hunger and need for communication.

The play has been extremely popular with audiences and has been translated into Spanish, Catalan, French, Hebrew and German.

"Susan Yankowitz's *Night Sky* is a rare thing: a play with a mind. It is also about the mind as universe, where language is internal astronomy. It shows us that more than hearts can be broken."
– *Variety*

"A moving and poetic experience. Like the sky, it is a play of seemingly infinite depth."
– *Los Angeles Times*

CPSIA information can be obtained
at www.ICGtesting.com
Printed in the USA
BVHW042351200520
579863BV00006B/425